Trouble At SUGAR DIP WELL

by Esther Pearl Watson

Houghton Mifflin Company
Boston 2002

For Lili

www.houghtonmifflinbooks.com

The text of this book is set in Bookman Medium.
The illustrations are acrylic and colored pencil on paper.

Library of Congress Cataloging-in-Publication Data

Watson, Esther.
Trouble at Sugar Dip Well / written and illustrated by Esther Pearl Watson.
p. cm.
Summary: Cowgirl Jules and her clever horse Gertie save the townsfolk when Mean
Bulldog Pike and his greedy horse Bullet escape from jail and steal the water supply.
ISBN 0-618-11863-2
[1. Cowgirls — Fiction. 2. Robbers and outlaws — Fiction.
3. West (U.S.) — Fiction. 4. Humorous stories.] I. Title.
PZ7.W3267 Tr 2002
[E]—dc21   00-050036

Printed in Singapore
TWP 10 9 8 7 6 5 4 3 2 1

Out in the brown and dusty West lived a cowgirl named Jules, who was genuine like leather, strong like licorice. Her horse, Gertie, could sing, dance, cook, make a mean cup of coffee, multiply, divide, and speak three languages. Shoot, they were ten-gallon heroes with bull's-eye talent.

One day the sun beat down so hot that it left the little town of Knot Belly as thirsty as a cactus. With the help of their buffalo buddy, Little Horn, Jules and Gertie rounded up buckets and filled them with fresh water from the Sugar Dip Well.

Jules sang a lemon-aid ditty and Gertie danced a sugary sweet twist.
Together they whipped up a cool breeze in a glass with ice and cubes.
The dusty town folks were as happy as catfish in a creek. Yikki Yea!

Watching from inside the stuffy county jail, Mean Bulldog Pike and his greedy horse, Bullet, frowned. Foul ideas rotted underneath their smelly hats. Those two crooks boiled up a scheme that would forever wash out those dance-happy heroes and make barrels of money!

Pike and Bullet sawed off the jail bars and slipped out of that crook-castle like slick eels.

Suddenly Little Horn busted into Jules and Gertie's do-si-do and stopped them on a dime. Pike and Bullet were gone!

Lickety-split, Gertie tracked those rustlers' trail across town and right to Ol' Sugar Dip, where the water had been robbed and the well left dry!

But Jules and Gertie were as tough as hide. Those heroes, brave and strong, climbed into the dark with stone-crushing courage.

On the muddy bottom, Pike and Bullet's trail vanished into the wall.

Well, those jailbirds couldn't outwit Gertie's four-ace brain! She found their secret door . . .

and those bold gals broke into Pike and Bullet's hideout.

Hidden around the bend, Mean Bulldog Pike and his weasel of a horse waited for that gal-puncher and her brainy sidekick to fall into their soggy trap.

Pike pulled the lever and released all the town's hidden water in
one bull-chaser of a wave. Water, lightning fast, rushed in after
Jules and Gertie!

That angry wave picked up those brave gals and carried them off.

Just in time, Gertie saddled onto one of the many passing barrels.
But in that big rinse, she didn't notice that her barrel was filled
with dynamite or that Pike's hand was lighting the fuse.

When that wave settled down, deep underground, Jules wrestled herself right-side up. All of a sudden she saw her buddy dancing on a barrel of burning dynamite!

Meanwhile, back at the exit of the underground hideout, Pike and Bullet quickly jumped out of their barrels and loaded up their carts with stolen water. In the crack of a whip, Jules and Gertie would go up in smoke! Then no one could save Knot Belly from Pike and Bullet's money-making schemes. Those outlaws rode off, spitting and slobbering all over themselves with excitement.

Back in town, the sun had near burnt the hide and hair off the town folks. And just when the West thought things couldn't get more ugly, Pike and Bullet rode into town. Mean Bulldog Pike and his cheat of a horse lined folks up like dominoes and made them pay dollar after dollar for an itty-bitty sip of cool, fresh water.

Bullet bullied Little Horn rough,

and Pike pushed him hard until his tiny sip splashed and spilled all over the ground.

Those two thirst cheaters laughed in a one-for-all fix.

Little Horn knew only to watch down the Sugar Dip Well for Jules and Gertie and hope that they'd return. Instead, a tumbling puff of black smoke rose out of the well. Little Horn feared his ten-gallon heroes were gone, and his tiny heart broke. It hurt painful like a pinch.

But that wasn't the end of these cow gals. Even though the walls of the underground hideout crumbled down and that gawl-darned water climbed up, Jules and Gertie fought their way back to the way they'd come in. But the secret entrance was blocked!

Quickly, Gertie pitched the heavy rocks aside and Jules picked the lock of the jammed door.

Right then the whole town of Knot Belly shook like a rattle on a rattlesnake . . .

and Jules and Gertie rode out of the Sugar Dip Well like a couple of sodbusters!

Water showered everywhere and cooled the town off. Just before Little Horn was swept away like a missing puzzle piece, Gertie rounded him up and set him down safe as sasparilla.

Then Gertie caught up with those outlaws
and gave them a double dose of her

up-down

left-right

cha-cha

spin cycle

hot lead

Very Bad Medicine!

And Jules lassoed those bullies. She buttered 'em and churned 'em and a busted 'em out of those barrels.

Scratchy Pike and his blistery horse were booted right back into that stuffy county jail. Jules and Gertie wrung the town's waters back into the Sugar Dip well, mopped up the stolen money, and returned it to soggy town folks with a song. One thing Little Horn knew for sure, he didn't have to worry about Pike and Bullet with Jules and Gertie around!

And so the West was soothed to the sound of a hero's do-si-do
and cooled off with a glass of ice-cold lemon-aid. A victory jubilee.

Yikki Yea!